TITCH

by PAT HUTCHINS

MACMILLAN PUBLISHING CO., INC.
New York

J

H

Macmillan Publishing Co., Inc., 866 Third Avenue, New York, N.Y. 10022
Collier Macmillan Canada Ltd. ISBN 0-02-745880-6
Library of Congress catalog card number: 77-146622
Printed in the United States of America

10   9   8   7   6

The art was prepared in four colors—black pen-and-ink line drawings
and separate overlays for yellow, red and blue, with benday tones to
make green, brown, orange, and gray. The text is set in Folio Light.

For Darren

Titch was little.

His sister Mary
was a bit bigger.

And his brother Pete
was a lot bigger.

Pete had a great big bike.

Mary had a big bike.

And Titch had a little tricycle.

Pete had a kite
that flew high
above the trees.

Mary had a kite
that flew high
above the houses.

And Titch had a pinwheel
that he held in his hand.

Pete had a big drum.

Mary had a trumpet.

And Titch had
a little wooden whistle.

Pete had a big saw.

Mary had a big hammer.

And Titch held the nails.

Pete had a big spade.

Mary had a fat flowerpot.

But Titch had the tiny seed.

And Titch's seed grew

and grew

and grew.